BEAVERBROOK

BEAVERBROOK

THE TALE

OF

THE

Firebird

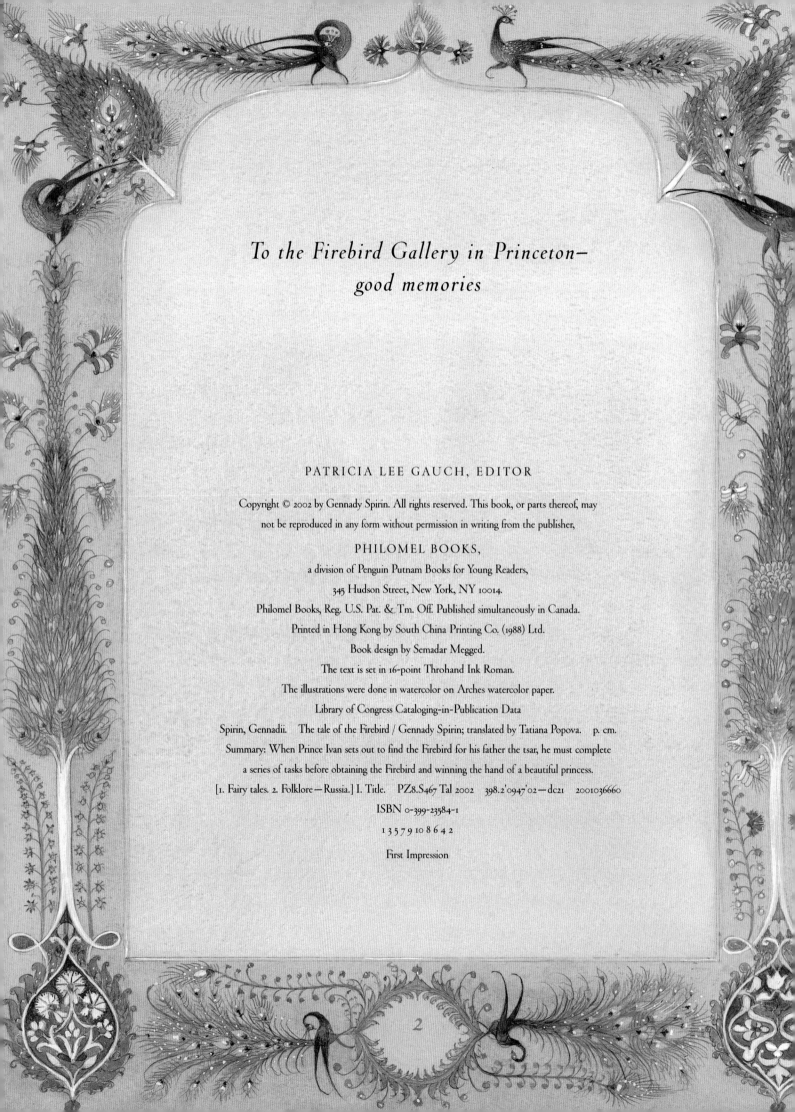

To the Firebird Gallery in Princeton—
good memories

PATRICIA LEE GAUCH, EDITOR

Copyright © 2002 by Gennady Spirin. All rights reserved. This book, or parts thereof, may
not be reproduced in any form without permission in writing from the publisher,

PHILOMEL BOOKS,

a division of Penguin Putnam Books for Young Readers,

345 Hudson Street, New York, NY 10014.

Philomel Books, Reg. U.S. Pat. & Tm. Off. Published simultaneously in Canada.

Printed in Hong Kong by South China Printing Co. (1988) Ltd.

Book design by Semadar Megged.

The text is set in 16-point Throhand Ink Roman.

The illustrations were done in watercolor on Arches watercolor paper.

Library of Congress Cataloging-in-Publication Data

Spirin, Gennadii.   The tale of the Firebird / Gennady Spirin; translated by Tatiana Popova.   p. cm.

Summary: When Prince Ivan sets out to find the Firebird for his father the tsar, he must complete

a series of tasks before obtaining the Firebird and winning the hand of a beautiful princess.

[1. Fairy tales. 2. Folklore—Russia.] I. Title.   PZ8.S467 Tal 2002   398.2'0947'02—dc21   2001036660

ISBN 0-399-23584-1

1 3 5 7 9 10 8 6 4 2

First Impression

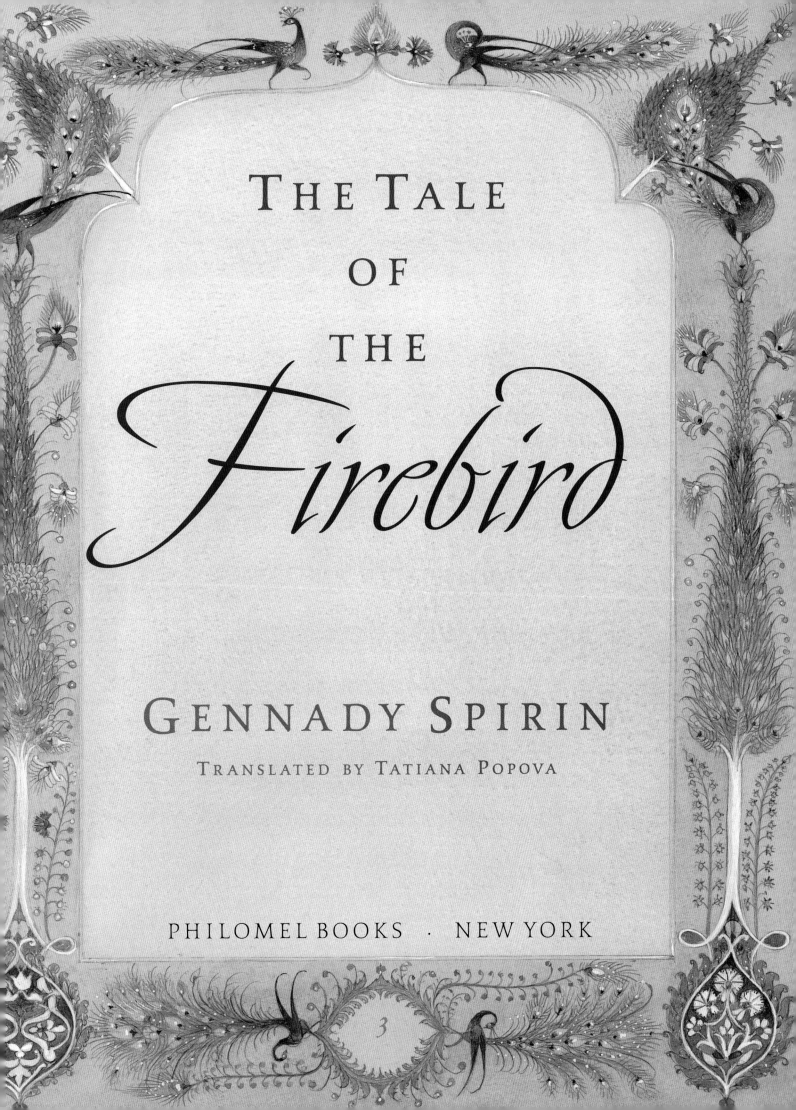

THE TALE

OF

THE

Firebird

GENNADY SPIRIN

TRANSLATED BY TATIANA POPOVA

PHILOMEL BOOKS · NEW YORK

3

Once upon a time, in a faraway kingdom, lived the great ruler Tsar Vasilyi. He had three sons, and the youngest was named Ivan-Tsarevitch.

The Tsar's greatest pride was his garden, filled with exotic trees, and in the center of this garden was the prize of his kingdom: a tree with golden apples.

One day the Tsar's gardener came to report that someone had been stealing the fruits of the golden apple tree! Every night there were fewer apples left. Determined to catch the thief, the Tsar ordered his three sons to watch his precious garden through the night.

The eldest son was in charge on the first night, but he fell

asleep and came back to his father the next day with nothing
to report. The second son tried to watch the garden on the
second night, but he, too, fell asleep and saw nothing.

On the third night, the youngest, Ivan-Tsarevitch, was
sent to the garden. He watched until midnight without
falling asleep. Just as his eyes were about to close, a sudden
flash of light illuminated the entire garden.

A Firebird!

As soon as the Firebird landed on the golden tree, Ivan-
Tsarevitch grabbed for his tail. That would stop him. But it
didn't! The Firebird flew away, leaving Ivan-Tsarevitch with
a single glowing feather in his hand.

The Tsar was amazed when he saw the miraculous light of the Firebird's feather. "I must have this Firebird!" he said. "Saddle your horses, my dear sons. Whichever of you can catch the Firebird will have half my kingdom as a reward!"

So the three sons rode off, each going his own way. Whether it was a long way or a short way, we don't know.

Ivan-Tsarevitch rode to the edge of a primeval forest, where he met a big gray wolf. "You cannot get the Firebird

without me, Ivan-Tsarevitch," the wolf said. "Leave your horse here and saddle me instead. You spared my children in the Tsar's wolf hunt last year, so now I will be your servant and your guide."

So Ivan-Tsarevitch climbed up on the wolf's back. The wolf made a great leap—all the way up to the birds in the sky. They flew over woods and mountains, over wide rivers, so high that it took Ivan-Tsarevitch's breath away.

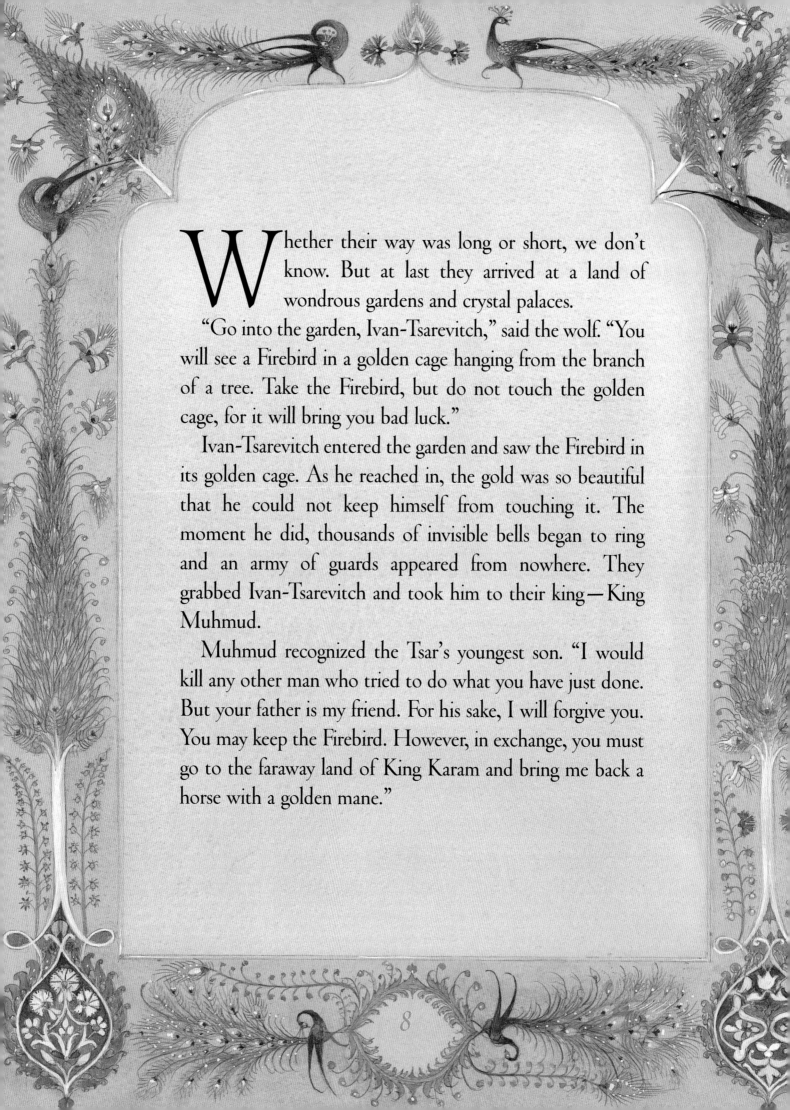

Whether their way was long or short, we don't know. But at last they arrived at a land of wondrous gardens and crystal palaces.

"Go into the garden, Ivan-Tsarevitch," said the wolf. "You will see a Firebird in a golden cage hanging from the branch of a tree. Take the Firebird, but do not touch the golden cage, for it will bring you bad luck."

Ivan-Tsarevitch entered the garden and saw the Firebird in its golden cage. As he reached in, the gold was so beautiful that he could not keep himself from touching it. The moment he did, thousands of invisible bells began to ring and an army of guards appeared from nowhere. They grabbed Ivan-Tsarevitch and took him to their king — King Muhmud.

Muhmud recognized the Tsar's youngest son. "I would kill any other man who tried to do what you have just done. But your father is my friend. For his sake, I will forgive you. You may keep the Firebird. However, in exchange, you must go to the faraway land of King Karam and bring me back a horse with a golden mane."

Ivan-Tsarevitch went back to his wolf and told him what King Muhmud had said. "Don't worry, Ivan-Tsarevitch," said the gray wolf. "I can help you find this horse. But I tell you, next time, do not disobey me!"

So Ivan-Tsarevitch saddled the wolf again, and in three great leaps they had reached the sky and were soaring above the clouds. They flew over high mountains, deep seas, and enormous green lands.

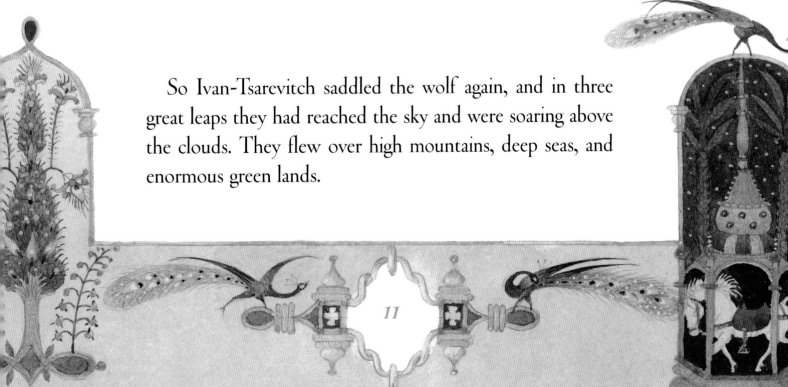

Finally they reached the kingdom of Karam, and the wolf gave Ivan-Tsarevitch his instructions. "Go into the king's garden, and you will see a horse grazing on the meadow. Take the horse by its golden mane and bring it here, but do not touch its harness, for it will bring you bad luck."

Ivan-Tsarevitch did everything as the wolf told him, but when he saw the harness, its golden beauty was so fascinating that he could not resist the temptation to touch it. As soon as he did, there was a sound of thousands of invisible bells and at the same moment, the guards appeared. They brought Ivan-Tsarevitch to see King Karam.

King Karam looked at Ivan-Tsarevitch with menacing eyes. "Who are you? Why do you want my horse?" Ivan-Tsarevitch told the king his story, holding back no secrets.

Karam said, "I will give you this horse and his golden harness as a gift—but in return you must go to the kingdom beyond all other kingdoms, the kingdom of Koshchei the Immortal, and bring my sister, Yelena the Beautiful, back to me. Since her capture three years ago, my suffering has been endless. Many heroes have lost their heads on Koshchei's field on her account. May God help you! Go!"

Ivan-Tsarevitch came back to his wolf in low spirits and told him what had passed. "Don't despair, Ivan-Tsarevitch—a man can die but once," said the wolf. "Get ready to go on another journey. I know who can help us."

So Ivan-Tsarevitch saddled the gray wolf once again, and they rushed as fast as they could to the kingdom beyond all other kingdoms, the kingdom of Koshchei the Immortal. They flew over dark woods and impassable swamps.

"Now we are coming to the place where no human has ever set foot," said the gray wolf. "Baba Yaga the Wicked dwells here. If you want to find Yelena the Beautiful, you must do everything Baba Yaga tells you."

Ivan-Tsarevitch turned and saw a cottage that spun around on chicken feet in the middle of the dark forest. It spun so fast that he could not see the door to enter. After consulting with the wolf, Ivan-Tsarevitch stood before the cottage and shouted, "Little hut, little hut, show your front to me and your back to the woods!"

The cottage immediately stopped spinning and settled down on its chicken feet with its door facing Ivan-Tsarevitch. He was about to knock at the door when he heard a great thunderclap and Baba Yaga the Wicked suddenly appeared.

"Why have you come to visit me, Ivan-Tsarevitch?" she cackled. "I think I know. I will help you — if you are brave!" Baba Yaga gave a shout, and from all corners of the forest,

creatures came running: satyrs, monsters, and other beasts.
Baba Yaga ordered them to build a fire and put on a huge
cauldron of magical waters and herbs. When this witch's
brew began to boil, she ordered Ivan-Tsarevitch to take off
his clothes and bathe himself in the bubbling cauldron.

Ivan-Tsarevitch crossed himself . . . and jumped in.

And then—a miracle! Instead of being boiled like a
shrimp, Ivan-Tsarevitch found himself in the cool water of
a forest lake. In the middle of the lake was a little island
covered with sedge and moss, and deep in the moss was a
glimmer of something shining.

He pushed the sedge away. There was a dazzling sword.

As soon as Ivan-Tsarevitch touched its hilt, a magical strength came to him.

Ivan-Tsarevitch stood up and found himself at the edge of the forest, still holding the magical sword. His faithful wolf was waiting for him, all ready with his clothes.

"You did a good job this time, Ivan-Tsarevitch," he said.

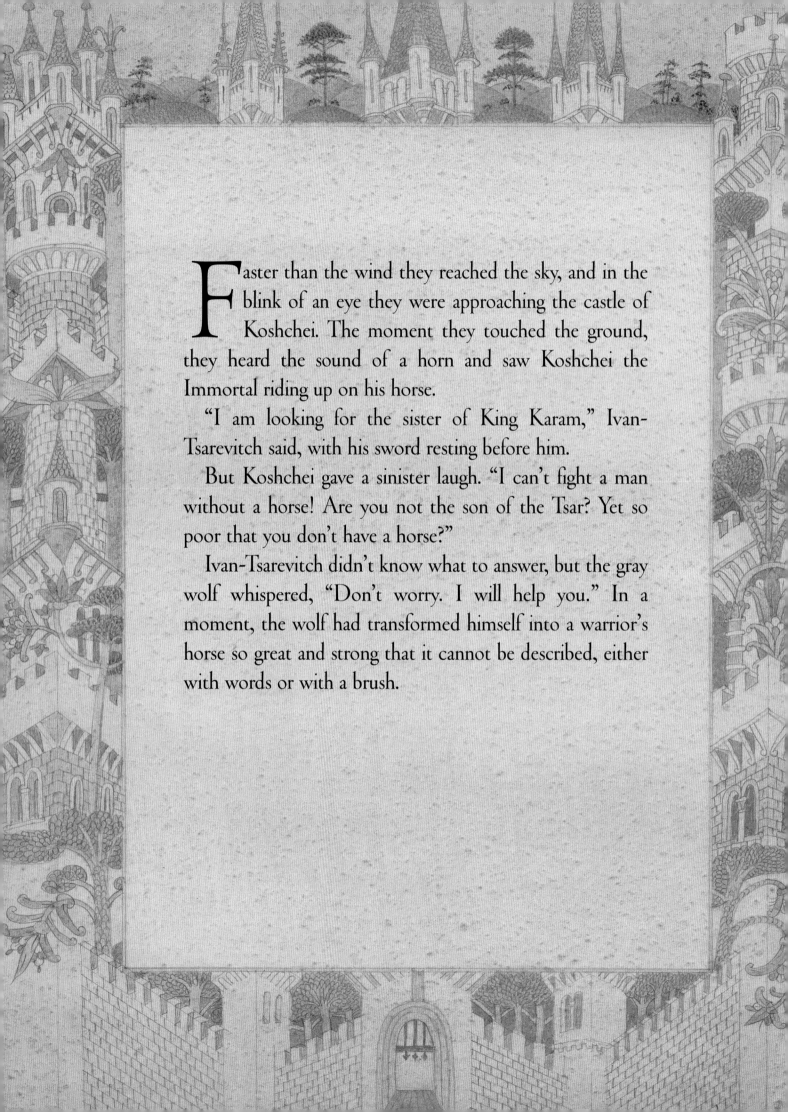

Faster than the wind they reached the sky, and in the blink of an eye they were approaching the castle of Koshchei. The moment they touched the ground, they heard the sound of a horn and saw Koshchei the Immortal riding up on his horse.

"I am looking for the sister of King Karam," Ivan-Tsarevitch said, with his sword resting before him.

But Koshchei gave a sinister laugh. "I can't fight a man without a horse! Are you not the son of the Tsar? Yet so poor that you don't have a horse?"

Ivan-Tsarevitch didn't know what to answer, but the gray wolf whispered, "Don't worry. I will help you." In a moment, the wolf had transformed himself into a warrior's horse so great and strong that it cannot be described, either with words or with a brush.

Koshchei the Immortal stopped laughing. Ivan-Tsarevitch mounted the great warrior horse and drew his magical sword. The battle began.

Ten times they drew their swords and charged at each other. But their strengths were evenly matched, and neither could win.

Then, just as Ivan-Tsarevitch was about to make another

charge, he spotted Yelena the Beautiful. Her beauty gave him a jolt of power, and his strength was suddenly doubled. Ivan-Tsarevitch attacked Koshchei once more with his magical sword and struck him with a final, deadly blow.

That was the end of the evil Koshchei, for evil cannot be immortal. Only love can be immortal.

Yelena the Beautiful and Ivan-Tsarevitch fell in love at first sight. Yelena the Beautiful made a wreath of field flowers and crowned Ivan-Tsarevitch. Then they saddled the mighty warrior horse, and in less than a moment, they had arrived at the kingdom of Karam.

Karam ran out of his palace to meet them. Tears streamed from his eyes at the sight of his beloved sister. He embraced her and Ivan-Tsarevitch together, saying, "I bless your love, my dear children. I am giving my kingdom to you, Ivan-Tsarevitch, and I want you to be its ruler when I am old."

Ivan-Tsarevitch thanked Karam for his generous gifts and went off to fulfill the rest of his promises. He saddled the horse with the golden mane for Yelena and mounted his warrior horse beside her.

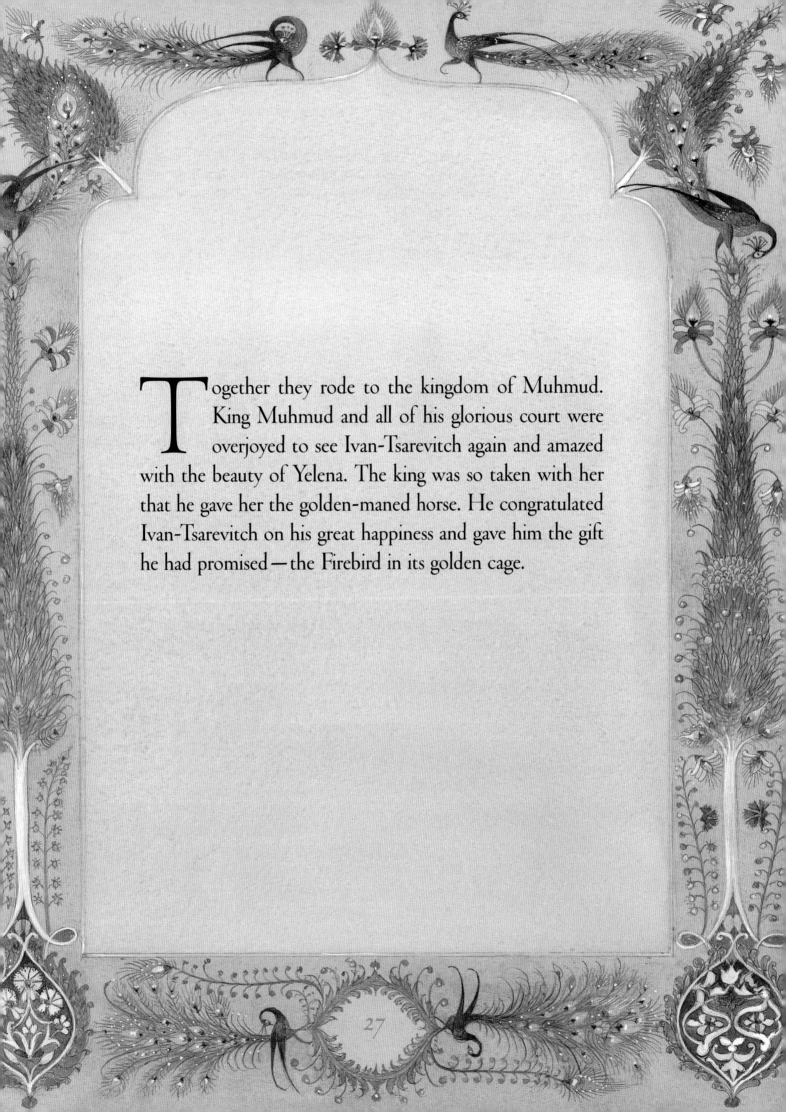

Together they rode to the kingdom of Muhmud. King Muhmud and all of his glorious court were overjoyed to see Ivan-Tsarevitch again and amazed with the beauty of Yelena. The king was so taken with her that he gave her the golden-maned horse. He congratulated Ivan-Tsarevitch on his great happiness and gave him the gift he had promised—the Firebird in its golden cage.

When Ivan-Tsarevitch and Yelena the Beautiful returned to the king's stables, they found that the warrior horse had transformed itself back into a gray wolf once again. "Here my help ends, Ivan-Tsarevitch. Be happy!" Ivan-Tsarevitch thanked him, and the wolf vanished into the dark woods.

Tsar Vasilyi was very happy to see his beloved son with
Yelena the Beautiful and all the kingly gifts they had been
given. The wedding was declared and the Tsar gave a feast for
everyone in the kingdom, brightened by the light of the

Firebird. For many, many years afterward, the people in that part of the world still talked of the wedding feast of the Tsar's youngest son and of the magical power and beauty of the Firebird.

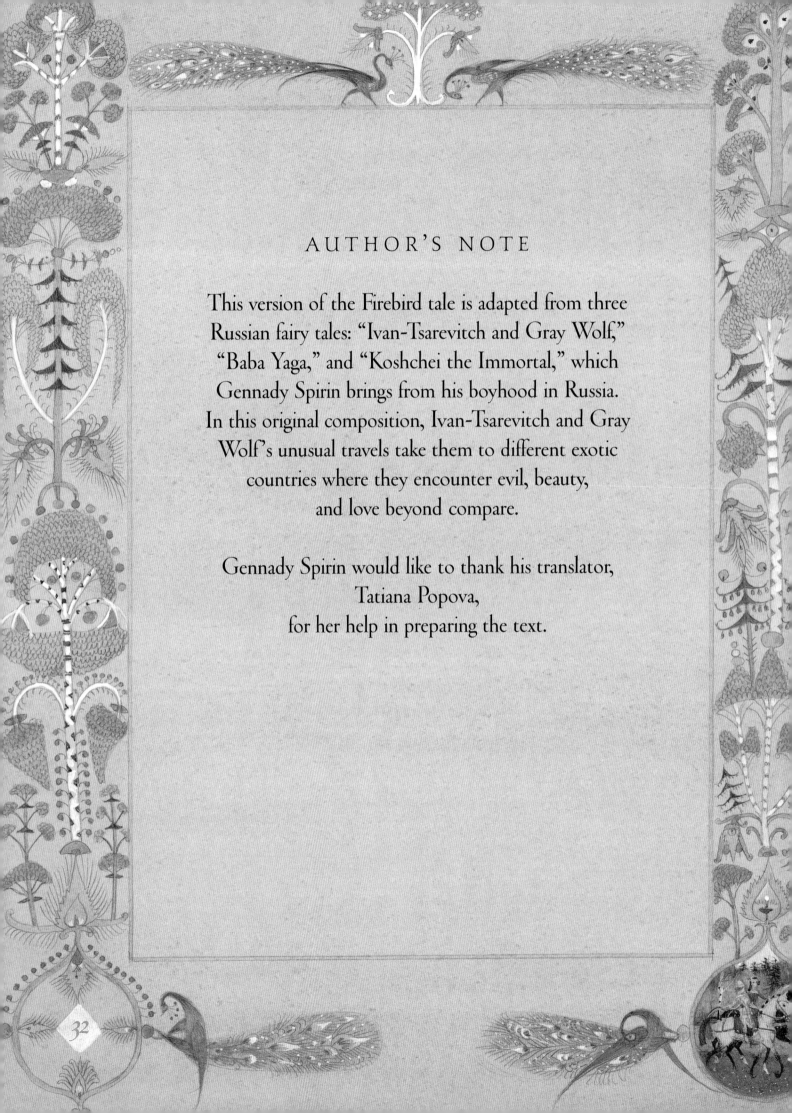

AUTHOR'S NOTE

This version of the Firebird tale is adapted from three
Russian fairy tales: "Ivan-Tsarevitch and Gray Wolf,"
"Baba Yaga," and "Koshchei the Immortal," which
Gennady Spirin brings from his boyhood in Russia.
In this original composition, Ivan-Tsarevitch and Gray
Wolf's unusual travels take them to different exotic
countries where they encounter evil, beauty,
and love beyond compare.

Gennady Spirin would like to thank his translator,
Tatiana Popova,
for her help in preparing the text.